Swimming with Sharks

ALSO IN THE *Gym Shorts* SERIES

Basketball Bats

Goof-Off Goalie

SWIMMING WITH SHARKS

Betty Hicks

Illustrated by Adam McCauley

ROARING BROOK PRESS
NEW YORK

Many thanks to expert swimmers JJ Marus and Leigh Abraham
for taking the time to read my manuscript and for giving me so many
valuable suggestions. I am also grateful to Sherry Marus, "swim mom"
extraordinaire, for listening to me and validating my plot ideas in the
book's earliest stages. —B. H.

Published by Roaring Brook Press
Roaring Brook Press is a division of
Holtzbrinck Publishing Holdings Limited Partnership
175 Fifth Avenue, New York, New York 10010
www.roaringbrookpress.com

Library of Congress Cataloging-in-Publication Data
Hicks, Betty.
Swimming with Sharks / Betty Hicks ; illustrated by Adam McCauley. — 1st ed.
p. cm. — (Gym shorts ; 3)
Summary: Rita tries to improve her times and flip turns as she struggles to decide
whether to remain the best swimmer on the Dolphins team or the worst on the
Sharks team, where she could be with her friends.
ISBN-13: 978-1-59643-245-1   ISBN-10: 1-59643-245-4
[1. Swimming—Fiction. 2. Perseverance (Ethics)—Fiction. 3. Self-realization—
Fiction.] I. McCauley, Adam, ill. II. Title.
PZ7.H53155Swi 2008   [Fic]—dc22   2008011126

Book design by Jennifer Browne
Printed in the United States of America   First Edition September 2008
2   4   6   8   10   9   7   5   3   1

For Addison

CONTENTS

1. You're a Dolphin   1
2. Stuff That Stinks   6
3. Break a Leg   9
4. Against the Law   14
5. Lucky Goose   18
6. Quitter   24
7. Flip Flop   28
8. Pretzels and Raisins   34
9. Zig or Zag?   38
10. Just Barely   43
11. No Clip Flip   47

You're a Dolphin!

The worst day of Rita's life was the day she became a dolphin.

A day like that should have been stamped with a warning label:

BEWARE!
TODAY WILL BE BAD

But, there had been no warning. None.

Rita had popped out of bed. She couldn't wait to put on her brand-new warm-up suit—the purple one with ruffles. She couldn't stop smiling. She was one hundred percent ready to try out for the swim team!

Even after Rita got to the pool, there was *still* no warning. It felt like a *good* day.

Rita did a perfect racing dive. She loved how the water felt as her body sliced through it. Bubbles streamed all over her, welcoming her to a smooth underwater world.

When she'd swum two laps, Miss York punched Rita's time on her stop watch.

"Rita," she said. "You're a Dolphin!"

"Woo hoo!" cheered Rita. She lifted her hands into the air and twirled like a dancer.

Dolphins, thought Rita, *are very cool fish.* They're sleek, smart, friendly, fast. And, soooo graceful. She glided over and took her place beside two other kids that Miss York had named Dolphins.

Rita's friends, Rocky, Jazz, and Henry stood across from her, dripping pool water.

Rita waited for Miss York to tell them that they were Dolphins, too.

Miss York pointed to Jazz. "You're a Shark."

A Shark? thought Rita. *Jazz is a Shark? Not a Dolphin?* She tilted her head and banged it with her hand. Was water stuck in her ear?

"Henry," announced Miss York. "You're a Shark, too."

Jazz and Henry hurried over to form a new group. Rita's mouth fell open. Her towel slid off her shoulders and landed in the water that had puddled at her feet.

"Rocky," said Miss York. She checked his name off on her clipboard. "Shark."

Rita's heart felt as if someone was squeezing it. It needed room to beat, but there wasn't any.

She picked up her drippy towel and pulled it tight around her shoulders.

Miss York assigned five more people. "Shark. Dolphin. Dolphin. Shark. Shark." Rita watched all her

friends become Sharks. She didn't know a single kid
who was a Dolphin. Not one. She elbowed the boy
next to her. "How do I get to be a Shark?"

"Ow," said the boy. He rubbed his arm.

"Sorry," said Rita. She hadn't meant to hurt him.
Sometimes her jabs got carried away.

Before he could answer, Miss York explained, "Sharks swam faster times, so they'll form one team. Dolphins," Miss York smiled at Rita's group, "will make up a second team. At swim meets, each team competes against teams that swim like they do."

Oh! Rita sighed with relief. She'd be at the same meets as her friends. They'd just swim different races.

Miss York passed out schedules.

Rita did a little wiggle dance with her hips. *Dolphins have style*, she thought.

Rita looked at the schedule. Dolphin Meets, she read on one side—*Thursdays*. She turned it over. Shark Meets—*Saturdays*.

No way.

Dolphins are stupid, thought Rita.

STUFF THAT STINKS

Most of the time, Rita moved like a dancer. But today, she stood like a statue.

She was a Dolphin. All her friends were Sharks.

Henry hurried over to her. Jazz and Rocky followed.

"This stinks!" exclaimed Henry. "You should be on the best team." He swept his arm in a circle. "With us!"

Jazz and Rocky nodded.

"Don't worry," said Rocky. "You'll be a Shark in no time."

"Ha!" said Rita.

Rocky was named after the boxer—the one in the movie who never quit.

"All you have to do," said Jazz, "is speed up your turns."

"Turns?" echoed Rita. Jazz knew stuff about everything, but turns? What was wrong with her turns?

"Flip turns," said Henry. "You have to learn how to do a flip turn."

"Yuck," said Rita. She hated flip turns. She just couldn't do them. She ended up twisted. Upside down with water up her nose. Every time.

Could she *learn* to do one? No. She turned and playfully pushed Henry into the pool.

"No pushing!" warned Miss York.

Rocky jumped in. Next, Jazz bombed the water with her best cannon ball.

"Flip turns stink!" yelled Rita.

Henry popped up. "Homework stinks!" he cried, then splashed Rocky.

"Rotten eggs stink!" exclaimed Jazz, wrinkling her nose.

"Henry's feet stink!" shouted Rocky.

Henry grabbed Rocky's head and pushed it under the water.

"No dunking!" shouted Miss York.

Rita splashed Henry.

Henry dove under the water and grabbed Rita's ankle. She laughed and kicked his wrist.

Rita heard Henry shout, *"Ouch!"* under water. With bubbles, it sounded like *blouch!*

Rita wished she were a Shark.

BREAK A LEG

Rita's first Dolphin meet was on Thursday.

It was thirty-three degrees outside. And raining.

Yuck, thought Rita.

She wanted to feel warm and loose—so she could swim her fastest time, ever.

So fast, that Miss York would have to make her a Shark.

Rita twisted the ruffley hem on her new purple warm-up jacket.

Two girls on the Dolphin team sat on the edge of the pool. Their feet dangled in the water. One of them had a million freckles. They whispered. And giggled.

Should Rita make friends with them? Why, she thought? After today, she hoped she wouldn't *be* on this team.

Most days, Rita twirled. She glided. But today, she paced. Back and forth.

The wall clock said 4:15.

Miss York had entered her in the 100 freestyle. When did her race start?

Seven boys hit the water for the 100 butterfly. The pool exploded with splashes. Cheers filled the giant building—bouncing off the metal rafters high above her head. The air felt tingly. It smelled like that stuff they used to clean pools.

Rita slipped off her flip-flops. She loved the plastic daisy between the toes. She wiggled out of her warm-

10

up suit. Her arms made wide circles in the air. She felt graceful, but strong. She could do this!

Rita knew that lots of swimmers used a grab start. Their fingers and toes curled over the edge of the starting block.

But she liked a track start. With one foot back. It felt better.

Should she try a grab start? Would it make her faster?

No. She shook her head.

What about her turn? Should she try a flip turn?

No. Her flip turns stank. Or was it stunk?

Stink. Stank. Stunk.

The clock said 4:25.

Her teammates huddled in a few small groups. Talking. Laughing.

Rita slid her flip-flops back on, then slumped onto a bench. Alone. She draped her towel over her shoulders.

She stretched her goggles around her head. Adjusted the elastic strap. Took them off again.

The clock said 4:35.

The inside of Rita's mouth felt drier than leftover toast. She wished she had a lemon drop. She wished her friends were here.

The clock said 4:36.

"Rita!" shouted Jazz.

Rita turned. She spotted Jazz, Henry, and Rocky! Goose had come, too. They all hurried over.

"Good luck!" cried Rocky and Henry.

"Break a leg," said Goose.

Jazz rolled her eyes. "That's what you say to an actor before his play starts. This," she swept her hands wide, "is a swim meet."

"Whatever." Goose shrugged. "It still means good luck." He smiled his famous goofball grin and shoved a grape Tootsie Pop at Rita. "Sorry it's not a lemon drop."

Rita loved lemon drops.

"Thanks!" said Rita.

"9 and 10 girls!" boomed a voice over the public address system. "100 freestyle!"

Rita froze. *That's me.*

"You'll win," said Rocky.

"Break a leg," said Jazz.

Against the Law

"9 and 10 girls!" repeated the loud speaker.

Rita stuffed Goose's Tootsie Pop in her pocket. She flung off her jacket and pitched her flip-flops under the bench. Hurrying to the starting block, she stuffed her frizzy hair under a swim cap.

Rita dried the starting block with her towel. She adjusted her goggles. Just like Miss York had showed her.

Then she took her stance and breathed deeply. Miss York gave her a thumbs up.

"Swimmers take your marks!"

"*Beep!*"

The sound of the starter sent Rita's body diving through the air. She hit the water clean. Her feet began to kick. Her arms reached. One arm. Then the other. Pulling. Hard.

Rita felt great. She watched one hand slice into the water. Then the other. Bubbles streamed up each arm. She turned her head to breathe.

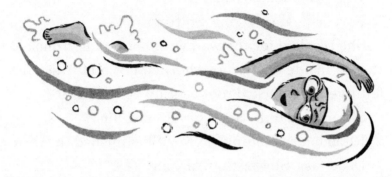

The swimmer in the next lane was ahead of her!

Pull harder, Rita told herself. *Faster.*

Should she try a flip turn?

No way.

She'd drown. Water would go up her nose.

When does a flip turn start? she asked herself, pulling forward with her right arm.

Rita was closing in on the turn.

Do it! Go for it!

Be a Shark!

Rita dropped one shoulder. She drove her head

toward her knees. Fast. Flip. Her feet should land on the wall. Where was the wall?

Her feet touched nothing but water. No wall.

Water flooded her nose.

Rita came up gagging. Spitting.

She reached for the wall with her hands. Touched it. The inside of her nose burned hot and fizzy. She felt like she'd sucked root beer up her nose.

She should quit. She'd never catch up.

Rita kept swimming anyway. She finished the race. Dead last. Slower than anyone.

"Don't worry," said Miss York. "Flip turns are hard. You'll get better."

Jazz and Goose faked their best smiles.

"She won't give up," said Rocky.

Henry nudged her arm and said, "Your dive was good." Then he shoved his hands in his pockets and studied his feet.

Rita stayed in the locker room until everyone had gone home. Then she went outside to wait for her dad to pick her up.

The air felt like liquid ice. It was freezing cold and raining.

She pulled her hood over her wet hair. It had frizzed out of control. Where was her dad? Why had she decided to swim in winter? Why wasn't there a law against flip turns?

Rita clenched her teeth. She flung the hood back off of her hair.

She hoped it got icicles in it. She hoped she got really sick.

LUCKY GOOSE

When Rita got home from school the next day, the sun was out. It was tons warmer.

Rita's younger sister, Tia, pedaled her bike around and around Rockford Court in front of their house.

"*Woo hoo!* Look at you!" exclaimed Rita.

Tia waved and grinned.

Her training wheels were off. Rita's older sister, Carly, ran beside Tia. She held the back of Tia's bike steady so it wouldn't tip over.

Rita remembered learning to ride a bike. It had been scary. And hard. She had a scar on her ankle to prove it.

"Tia!" Carly cried. "Next time around, I'm letting go. Okay?"

18

"No!" screamed Tia. She jerked her feet off the pedals. The bike wobbled wildly. Carly tried to hold it.

Tia, Carly, and the bike crashed.

Tia sprawled on the pavement under her bike. One wheel spun out of control. "Look what you did!" she wailed.

"What *I* did!" shrieked Carly. Blood seeped through the elbow of Carly's shirt sleeve.

Rita rushed over. She untangled Tia from the bike. "You okay?"

"I'm telling!" sobbed Tia. She ran for the house.

Carly shrugged. "That's what I get for helping."

"Are *you* okay?" Rita asked Carly.

"Fine," said Carly. She limped toward the house.

Rita sat down on the curb and stared at Tia's bike.

It lay twisted in an ugly heap.

Looking like one of Rita's flip turns.

Suddenly Rita felt like the bike. Crumpled.

All her friends were at the Shark meet. Doing flip turns at the speed of light.

Well. Not *all* her friends. Rita glanced at Goose's house. Goose lived on Rockford Court, across from Rita.

Jazz, Rocky, and Henry lived just around the corner, on Rockford Road. They had talked her into swimming.

Goose decided to play soccer instead. On a traveling team. He planned to become the greatest goalie on earth.

Lucky Goose.

Rita *liked* swimming. And diving. Especially diving. But she liked it outside, in the summer, with her friends.

Swimming and diving, she felt strong and graceful. But doing a flip turn, she felt awkward. Like someone else. Not Rita.

Should she quit the swim team?

Rita pulled a notebook out of her book bag. She'd make a list.

That's what Carly did when she couldn't decide on

a boyfriend. She made a list of what was good about them. And what was bad. If the bad list was longer than the good—*adios* boyfriend.

Adios meant good-bye in Spanish.

Rita wrote, SWIMMING – GOOD THINGS, at the top of a page. She chewed on the end of her pen. She wrote

1. I like how the bubbles feel
2. I like to dive
3. It's fun to do with my friends

But she *wasn't* diving. And she wasn't swimming with her friends.

She wadded up the page and threw it on the ground.

She wrote SWIMMING – BAD THINGS on a new page.

1. Flip turns stink
2. Being clumsy stinks
3. Being wet in winter stinks
4. Swim team suits don't have ruffles
5. I'm slower than my friends
6. I don't feel like me

Six things. The good list only had three.

A smile crept across Rita's face.

Adios swimming.

6

QUITTER

"Rita!" exclaimed Rocky. He waved his arms over his head. "You can't quit!"

"Watch me," said Rita. She had one hand on her hip. The other hand held open her front door. She faced Henry, Rocky, and Jazz.

When Rita hadn't run out to the van for swim practice, her friends had all crowded onto Rita's front porch.

Jazz's dad waited, parked in Rita's driveway. With the motor running. It was his turn to drive carpool.

Rita had answered the door and announced that she wasn't coming to practice. *Not today. Not ever.*

"Are you crazy?" said Henry. "You'll have nothing to do all week!"

"We'd miss you," said Jazz. "So *what* if our meets aren't on the same day? We still practice together."

"You're not a quitter," added Rocky.

"Ha!" said Rita. "You're the one that's not a quitter."

Rita began to hum the theme song from *Rocky*, the movie that had given Rocky his nickname. For never quitting.

Rita jogged in place as she hummed. She pumped her fists in the air. She twirled. Spinning made her feel graceful again.

"See!" said Jazz. "You're tough."

"Tougher than shark's teeth," said Henry.

Rita sagged. "Funny you should mention sharks," she said.

Henry groaned and threw up his hands.

Jazz's dad turned the van motor off.

"Look," said Rita in a small, quiet voice. "I'm not a Shark." She was feeling less tough by the minute. "And after my first meet, I may not even be a Dolphin." Rita slumped against her front door. "I bet I'm about to be a Turtle. Is there a Turtle team?"

"Rita," said Jazz, ignoring the question. She held up a tiny piece of yellow plastic. "I brought you something."

Rita stared at the small, weird thing in Jazz's hand.

"It's a nose clip. It'll keep water out of your nose," said Jazz. "For flip turns."

Rita never wanted to see another flip turn.

"It's yellow," said Jazz. "It matches the daisies on your flip-flops."

Rita laughed. "Thanks, Jazz. Really. But I'm not swimming anymore."

"Don't give up," begged Rocky.

"Yeah. Don't be a wimp," blurted Henry.

Rita knew Henry wasn't being mean. Quitting sports just freaked him out. Henry *had* to play sports.

Rita stretched up, standing tall. "I'm not a wimp. I'm just quitting. When something isn't you, it's okay to quit."

"But, Rita—"

"You guys should go now. Okay? Please. You'll be late. And . . . and . . . I'm sorry," she whispered. Then she eased the front door closed. Gently . . . but firmly.

Jazz's dad started the motor again.

Henry, Jazz, and Rocky walked slowly back to the waiting van.

Jazz dropped the nose clip. It sank into the grass.

Rita watched it all from behind a curtain.

FLIP FLOP

After breakfast on Saturday, Rita called to her sister, "Tia! Let's go ride your bike."

"I'm never riding that dumb bike again," yelled Tia as she slammed the back door. "I'm going to Jenny's house."

"Don't be a—" Rita almost said *wimp*, but stopped herself.

Rita's house felt empty.

Rita's older sister, Carly, had left at 6:00 a.m. to go snow skiing with her church group. Mom and Dad were slumped over the dining room table, filling out tax forms.

Goose was who-knows-where—playing soccer. Jazz, Henry, and Rocky were at a Shark meet—swimming their little hearts out.

Rita trudged upstairs to her room and flopped onto

her bed. She pulled her blanket up to her chin. What could *she* do?

Start her science project? Clean up her room? "Yuck."

Rita jerked the blanket over her face. She'd rather watch grass grow. Or paint dry.

She lowered the blanket and reached for the book she was reading—*A Wrinkle in Time*.

Meg, the girl in the book, was tough. Just like Rita.

Meg was stuck on a scary planet, searching for her father. To save him, she had to battle IT—a giant evil brain.

Rita read three chapters. Meg stood up to IT. She yelled at IT! Rita slammed the book shut.

How hard could it be to do a flip turn?

She rolled off the

bed and marched over to her computer. When she clicked on her mouse, five twirling ballet dancers filled the screen.

Then she logged online. Quickly, she typed a stream of words: *swimming flip turns how to.*

Dozens of items showed up.

How to Flip Turn, Flip, Don't Flop, Flip Turns Made Easy

Rita scrolled through the choices. She clicked on one that said, *"The Basic Flip Turn. Wow! Looks cool. Is it really needed?"*

Rita read, *"No, it's not needed."* She punched the air and cheered.

The next part said, *"Unless you want to win races."*

Rita stuck her tongue out at the computer.

She read one page. Then two, three, and four pages.

She read how to tuck your chin on your chest. How to keep your motion smooth. How to hold your breath.

She read: Stay on your side of the lane. Bring your knees to your chest. Start on your stomach. End on your back.

She scrolled down. There was more: Extend. Straighten. Rotate. Kick. Land.

"Aaaggh!!!" Rita screamed and yanked her hair with both hands.

She typed *headaches make them go away.*

A hundred ads popped up for pain relief. But not one of them said a word about flip turns.

Rita sighed and signed off.

She fell onto her bed. Maybe if she took a nap, her headache would go away. *"A nap!"* she moaned. How low could she sink!

Wait. Maybe she could sleep until she was old enough to go to college—a college with no swim team.

Rita curled up. She hugged her pillow. Maybe she could dream of a way to swim better.

"Look! Look at me!" cried Tia from the front yard.

Rita woke up and stumbled to her window. Tia was riding her bike. By herself. No training wheels. Around and around Rockford Court.

Fully awake, Rita raced downstairs, three steps at a time. "Tia!" she cried, flying out the front door. "Look at you! You did it! When? How? Wow!"

"Today. At Jenny's house." Tia's grin was as wide as her face. "On her bike. I learned. Watch!" Tia leaned low over her handle bars and pedaled faster.

Rita did a little wiggle dance with her hips. She clapped her hands and cheered, "*Woo hoo!*"

Twelve laps later, Tia stopped pedaling. She looked over at Rita and asked, "What are you doing?"

Rita knelt on her hands and knees. Carefully, she pushed aside blades of grass. "Looking for a piece of yellow plastic," she said.

PRETZELS AND RAISINS

Sunday, Rita asked her mom to take her and her friends to the YWCA. The big new one with an indoor pool.

Her friends were all so happy that Rita wanted to swim, they forgave her for shutting the door in their faces.

But Henry's parents said he had to do homework, Rocky was going to his grandmother's, and Goose had a soccer game.

That was fine. Jazz would be a great flip turn teacher.

When they got to the pool, Rita clipped the plastic yellow piece over her nose. She held up one foot to show Jazz how well it matched her flip-flops.

"Dolphins have style," said Rita.

"*You* have style," replied Jazz. "Ready to become a Shark?"

"First, I want to dive," answered Rita. She slipped off her flip-flops and walked to the spring board at the deep end of the pool. She climbed up on it and tip-toed gracefully to the end.

Rita paused near the edge. She held her arms out. Balanced on the toes of one foot, she twirled halfway around.

With her back to the water, Rita raised her arms above her head. Her heels hung off the end of the diving board. She arched her back. She sprang up and over. Her body entered the water exactly straight. Arms extended. Toes pointed. Almost no splash. A perfect back dive.

Bubbles swept over her. Rita loved bubbles.

"Wow!" said Jazz clapping. Then she shouted, "Let the flip turns begin!" and cannon balled into the water. Waves sloshed over the edge.

Jazz popped up. "Ready?" she asked.

No, thought Rita. She wanted to dive some more. But *yes*, she did want to learn flip turns.

For five minutes, Rita watched Jazz do flip turns. Jazz rolled into the wall like a ball. And away like a dart. Fast. Jazz was so small and quick, she made it look easy.

Rita tried it. Into the wall like a pretzel. Away like a flapping fish.

"I can't do this!" screamed Rita.

"Ha!" said Jazz. "You've almost got it!"

"Are you kidding?" said Rita.

"No water up your nose," Jazz pointed out.

"*Whoa!*" exclaimed Rita. It was true. No root beer fizz burning inside her face. The nose clip worked. "Thanks, Jazz."

"You're welcome." Jazz folded her arms across her chest. "Now, do it again."

"Meanie," grumbled Rita. But she tried again. Another flip turn.

She tried a hundred flip turns. She stayed in the water so long, her finger tips wrinkled into raisins.

But she *had* improved. A lot. A couple of times, she even felt graceful.

Would it be enough?

She'd know Thursday.

Thursday, she had another Dolphin meet.

ZIG OR ZAG?

"Rita," said Miss York. "You're wearing a nose clip."

Rita smiled and held up one foot to show Miss York that it matched her flip-flops. "I can do a flip turn," bragged Rita. She hoped it was true.

"Wonderful," said Miss York. "That will improve your time."

"Enough to be a Shark?" asked Rita.

Miss York studied the time chart on her clipboard. "Perhaps," she answered.

"Woo hoo!" Rita wiggled her hips.

"But Rita," warned Miss York. "You'll need to watch your stroke, too."

My stroke? thought Rita.

"At the last meet," said Miss York. "When you fell behind, you fought the water."

Fought the water?

"Your stroke should be smooth. Don't slap. Do it the way I showed everyone at practice. Remember?"

Rita didn't remember. Maybe she'd missed that practice.

"Pull in a zigzag curve. Like the letter S."

Zig! Zag! The letter S. Good grief! thought Rita.

"Girl's 100 freestyle!" boomed the loud speaker.

"You'll do fine." Miss York gently squeezed her arm. "Your racing dive is the best of anyone's. It'll give you a head start."

Rita stood on the starting block. She adjusted her goggles. She stared down at her lane. Number four. It

was divided by big, round, plastic lane lines. It seemed very long and narrow.

Her stomach churned. But her heart swelled—she had the best dive of anyone! Miss York had said so.

"Swimmers take your marks!"

"*Beep!*"

Rita sliced into the water like a knife. Shallow. Sharp. Clean. Lots of smooth bubbles. When the water began to slow her forward speed, she began her stroke. Smooth. Steady.

Was anyone ahead of her?

Don't look. Pull. Hands moving like an S. Or was it a Z?

Above the splashes, Rita heard people cheering. "Go Rita! Go Dolphins!"

The turn. It was coming. What if her nose clip fell off? What if she missed the wall? What if she came in last again?

Now, she thought. *Flip now*.

All of a sudden, lessons flooded Rita's brain. All the tips she'd read on the internet. All the things Jazz had shown her.

Start on your stomach. End on your back. Rotate. Don't twist your head. Extend. Which comes first? Where's the wall?

I can't do this!

I can do this!

I did it!

Rita wasn't sure what she'd done, but she knew she was swimming in the other direction. She knew her feet had gotten a solid push off the wall. And the bubbles felt great.

She stroked for the finish. Smooth. Even.

Rita touched the wall.

Her teammates cheered. They were pulling her out of the water. Hugging her. Shouting, "Rita, you won!"

I won! thought Rita.

Rita did her wiggle dance. She high-fived the girl with freckles.

"*Ow!*" said the girl.

When Rita slapped hands with the other teammates, she tried not to smack so hard.

She felt bubbly inside. She wished she knew their names.

This is the best! thought Rita. *Whoa!* Better than being a Shark? No way. Now she could be a Shark. Right?

JUST BARELY

"Woo hoo!" exclaimed Rita. She exploded out of the car. "I'm a Shark!"

Jazz, Rocky, and Henry cheered. They were waiting in her driveway. Rita had called them on her mom's cell phone as soon as she'd left the Dolphin meet.

Goose was there, too. He bowed low and extended

a Tootsie Pop to her. His idea of first prize.

"We knew you could do it!" cried Jazz.

Everyone exclaimed together, "Hooray for nose clips!" "Hooray for Sharks!"

"Hooray for Rita!"

Everyone crowded into Rita's kitchen for Oreos and milk. Rita liked to dunk hers. Rocky twisted the

wafers apart and licked the cream filling.

Jazz took three even bites out of each cookie. Henry jammed the whole thing in his mouth.

Goose peeled off his cream filling and wrapped it around a Tootsie Pop. It flopped onto the floor. He ate it anyway.

"Yuck," said Rita.

After their snack, everyone stood up to leave.

"See you Saturday!" cried Jazz.

Henry grinned. "At the *Shark* meet."

Rita waved good-bye. She twirled around her kitchen. She was a Shark! Miss York had said so.

Rita's faster time had made her a Shark. Just barely.

Saturday, Rita would swim in a Shark meet. She'd probably be the slowest. But who cared! She'd be with her friends.

All of a sudden, Rita remembered the Dolphins hugging her. She stopped twirling. She heard them cheering her name.

First place had felt amazing.

Like bubbles *inside*.

But Saturday, she'd be with her friends again. Winning didn't matter.

Did it?

No Clip Flip

Rita perched on a bench at the Shark meet. Her eyes focused on lane number three. Henry was swimming the 100 butterfly. His hands touched the finish a split

second before any other swimmer.

Rita jumped up and cheered. Then she sat back down, smiling for Henry.

She knew what winning felt like.

She thought about being one of the fastest Dolphins. Or one of the slowest Sharks.

She made two lists inside her head:

DOLPHINS
Good Thing - I'm the best swimmer
Bad Thing - I'm not with my friends

SHARKS
Good Thing - I'm with my friends
Bad Thing - I'm the worst swimmer

It was a tie.

Yuk, thought Rita. She wished she could be a Shark *and* win.

"Girl's 100 freestyle!" boomed the loud speaker.

Rita's stomach flipped.

"Go, Rita!" cried Rocky.

"You can do it!" whispered Jazz.

"Keep your stroke smooth," said Miss York.

"Good luck!" called Henry.

Rita gave them all a thumbs up. She stuffed her hair into her cap and stepped up onto the starter's block. She strapped on her goggles, adjusted her swim suit, and took her stance.

The lane looked longer. And more narrow. But she knew it couldn't be.

"On your marks."

"*Beep!*"

Rita pushed off. She stretched herself out. She hit the water exactly right. A perfect racing dive.

Maybe I can *win*, she thought.

Right arm pull. Left arm pull. Make the letter S.
Breathe. Kick. Stay smooth.

Get ready for the turn.

Hooray for the nose clip!

The nose clip!

Rita had forgotten to wear her nose clip!

Her mind screamed. *I can't do this!*

She heard shouts. Voices yelling, "Go, Rita! Go,

Sharks! You can do it!"

Rita's hand grazed the plastic lane line. She was too close to the lane divider. *Forget about it. Just flip.*

Rita tucked her head and rolled into her turn. She flipped.

She pushed off the wall. No wall.

Where was the wall?

Water flooded her nose! It burned.

Back up! Touch the wall. Keep swimming.

Rita wanted to swim all the way to China. That way, she wouldn't have to get out of the pool. She wouldn't have to learn how badly she'd lost the race.

Rita touched the finish. Rocky, Jazz, and Henry pulled her out of the pool. "Good try!" they shouted.

"How bad did I lose?" asked Rita.

"You did fine," said Jazz. She hugged Rita.

"You forgot your nose clip," said Rocky.

"No kidding," said Rita.

"Don't worry," said Miss York. She squeezed her shoulder. "You just need a little more practice."

"I came in last, didn't I?"

"Your dive was perfect," said Miss York.

"I brought you your towel," said Henry.

Rita dried off. She walked over and slumped onto the bench. She tried to watch the other races. But she couldn't.

Rocky and Jazz sat down next to Rita. Henry

joined them.

"No nose clip," said Jazz, pounding her palm with her fist. "I should have noticed."

"Your dive was better than anybody's," said Henry.

Rocky dropped three lemon drops into Rita's hand.

"Thanks," said Rita. She loved her friends.

She thought about her list—the one where good things and bad things had come out even. A tie. Were friends worth more than being the best?

Yeah, thought Rita. *They are.*

But still . . . Rita wished she could add just one more good thing to her Shark list. Something to totally break the tie.

Meanwhile, she'd keep working on her flip turn. And, she'd pin the nose clip to her warm-up jacket.

Rita was starting to feel good again.

"We're Sharks," she said proudly, punching Rocky.

"Yeah," said Henry and Jazz.

"Ow," said Rocky.

Together, they watched the last three races. Then Rocky stood up. "I'm helping Miss York take down the lane lines."

"What for?" asked Rita.

"The diving event," said Rocky.

"The diving event?" repeated Rita. "Shark meets have a diving event?"

"Yes," said Rocky.

"Right now?" asked Rita.

"Yes," said Rocky.

Why hadn't Miss York told her there was a diving event? Didn't she know Rita could dive?

No, thought Rita. She only knows I do a good racing dive. She's never seen my back dive. Or my jack-knife.

Rita bolted straight up. She twirled. She did a wig-

gle dance with her hips.

"Diving!" Jazz shouted. "Perfect! Why didn't we think—?"

"Yes!" yelled Henry.

"Rita," cried Rocky. "You should—"

But Rita didn't wait to hear him to finish. She had already added, *Good thing - Shark meets have diving*, to the list in her head.

No question—it broke the tie.

"Miss York!" called Rita. She had to find her. She had to show her that she could dive! At Shark meets. With her friends.

Rita hurried toward the other end of the pool.

Her flip-flops sounded as if they were clapping.